GATOR GUMBO
A SPICY-HOT TALE

CANDACE FLEMING   Pictures by SALLY ANNE LAMBERT

MELANIE KROUPA BOOKS · FARRAR STRAUS GIROUX · NEW YORK

For Jon Riley
—C.F.

For my children, Jonny and Katie, with love
—S.A.L.

Text copyright © 2004 by Candace Fleming
Illustrations copyright © 2004 by Sally Anne Lambert
All rights reserved
Distributed in Canada by Douglas & McIntyre Ltd.
Color separations by Chroma Graphics PTE Ltd.
Printed and bound in the United States of America by Berryville Graphics
Designed by Barbara Grzeslo
First edition, 2004
1 3 5 7 9 10 8 6 4 2

Library of Congress Cataloging-in-Publication Data
Fleming, Candace.
    Gator gumbo : a spicy-hot tale / by Candace Fleming ; pictures by
Sally Anne Lambert.— 1st ed.
        p.   cm.
    Summary: Tired of being tormented by bullies, a hungry old alligator
conjures up a way to add some special ingredients to his gumbo.
    ISBN 0-374-38050-3
    [1. Gumbo (Soup)—Fiction.   2. Alligators—Fiction.   3. Animals—
Fiction.]   I. Lambert, Sally Anne, ill.   II. Title.

PZ7.F59936 Gat 2004
[E]—dc21

                                                    2002029706

Let me tell you about Monsieur Gator.
Monsieur Gator, he lives down in the bayou, oh yes he do.
He lives on the edge of the swamp, uh-huh.
He has big claws, big teeth, and a big appetite, for sure.
But Monsieur Gator, he has a big problem, too.

You see, Monsieur Gator, he is getting old.
He is growing gray.
He is moving so-o-o

so-o-o

sl-o-o-o-w.
Hoo, I tell you, that gator moves slower than saw grass grows.
He moves slower than a snail with sore feet.

He moves so slow he cannot catch himself a taste of possum, or a bite of otter, or a whiff of stripe-tailed skunk.

And—oh ho!—them critters sure know it.

They sass Monsieur Gator.
They tease Monsieur Gator.
They pester Monsieur Gator something fierce.
They smarty-pants chant, "Try, try, as hard as you can! You can't catch us, 'cause you're an old man!"

Poor Monsieur Gator! At every meal he wipes away his tears and moans, *"Sacré Dieu!* Vegetables again."

One morning, as Monsieur Gator eats his thin breakfast of leaves, moss, and roots, Mademoiselle Possum comes tail-hanging from her tree.

"Yoo-hoo! Monsieur Gator!" she calls as she swings back and forth, just out of reach. "Am I lookin' tasty? Am I lookin' good?"

Monsieur Gator, he clamps tight his jaws and doesn't say a word.

So Monsieur Otter comes fur-shaking from the water to join in making fun.

"Oooh, I'm so scared!" he mocks. "Puhleeze, don't eat me!" And he sticks his paws in his ears, sticks his tongue out his mouth, and goes, "Nyah-nyah! Poo-poo!"

Monsieur Gator, he grinds hard his teeth, and still doesn't say a word.

So Madame Skunk comes sashaying from her log. She wiggles her
striped fanny, puff-puffs her perfume, and asks in a sugarcane voice, "Do I smell
like lunch?"

Then all three fall on their backs, kick up their feet, hold in their bellies,
and laugh till they cry.

"Hyeh! Hyeh! Hyeh!"

And Monsieur Gator, he gets hot . . .

red hot . . .

hotter than . . .

Gumbo!

"I'm gonna cook up some gumbo just like Maman used to make!" he cries.

So Monsieur Gator, he builds up a fire.
He sets a big pot over the flames.
He calls out to them slap-laughing critters, "Who's gonna fill this pot with water so I can cook up some gumbo?"

"I ain't," snickers Mademoiselle Possum.
"I ain't," snickers Monsieur Otter.
"I ain't," snickers Madame Skunk.
"Then I'll be doin' it myself," says Monsieur Gator.

Splash!
Pour!
Slop!

That water goes into the pot.

Pretty soon the water is bubbling hot and the steam is rising high.

Hoo, but them critters ain't never seen anything like it. They stop their guffawing. They take a step toward the pot.

"Mmm-mmm!" says Monsieur Gator. "*Almost* like Maman used to make. All this gumbo needs now is some claw-pinchin' fish. Who's gonna catch the crawdads?"

"I ain't," smirks Mademoiselle Possum.

"I ain't," smirks Monsieur Otter.

"I ain't," smirks Madame Skunk.

"Then I'll be doin' it myself," says Monsieur Gator.

Them crawdads go into the pot.

Well, it doesn't take long for that sweet smell of crawdads to up and tweak them critters' snouts. They step closer to the pot.

"Mmm-mmm!" says Monsieur Gator. "*Almost* like Maman used to make. All this gumbo needs now is some health-buildin' greens. Who's gonna pick the okra?"

"I ain't," snorts Mademoiselle Possum.

"I ain't," snorts Monsieur Otter.

"I ain't," snorts Madame Skunk.

"Then I'll be doin' it myself," says Monsieur Gator.

Pluc^k ! Slice!

That okra goes into the pot.

P^op !

The next thing you know, the smell of tangy okra and sweet crawdads sets them critters' lips smacking. They step a bit closer to the pot.

"Mmm-mmm!" says Monsieur Gator. "*Almost* like Maman used to make. All this gumbo needs now is some tongue-flamin' flavoring. Who's gonna grind the spices?"

"I ain't," sniffs Mademoiselle Possum.

"I ain't," sniffs Monsieur Otter.

"I ain't," sniffs Madame Skunk.

"Then I'll be doin' it myself," says Monsieur Gator.

Mince! Dice! Chop!

Them spices go into the pot.

And, you guessed it, the smell of sharp spices, tangy okra, and sweet crawdads gets them critters' bellies grumbling. They step even closer to the pot. "Mmm-mmm," says Monsieur Gator. "*Almost* like Maman used to make. All this gumbo needs now is some long-grained fluff. Who's gonna add the rice?"

"I ain't," snaps Mademoiselle Possum.
"I ain't," snaps Monsieur Otter.
"I ain't," snaps Madame Skunk.
"Then I'll be doin' it myself," says Monsieur Gator.

Pour!
Scrape!
Glop!

That rice goes into the pot.

Well, I tell you, there ain't nothing like the smell of white rice, sharp spices, tangy okra, and sweet crawdads. The savorous aroma of it all drives them critters so wild they rush right to the edge of that pot.

"Mmm-mmm," says Monsieur Gator. "*Almost* like Maman used to make. All this gumbo needs now is some hungry folks. Who's gonna help eat it?"

"**Me! Me!**" cries Mademoiselle Possum.

"**Me! Me!**" cries Monsieur Otter.

"**Me! Me!**" cries Madame Skunk.

"Humph," says Monsieur Gator. "I filled the pot, and I caught the crawdads. I picked the okra and ground up the spices. Heck, I even added the rice. So now I'm gonna eat this gumbo all by myself."

And he pulls out a big, big spoon and he dips it deep, deep into that gumbo.

"Just one taste," begs Mademoiselle Possum.
"One taste, puhleeze," begs Monsieur Otter.
"One taste and we won't tease you no more," promises Madame Skunk.
"One taste?" asks Monsieur Gator. "Is that all?"

"Yes! Yes! Yes!" cry them critters.

"Well, I suppose . . ." says Monsieur Gator.

Them animals go into the pot.
And Monsieur Gator, he sniffs that delicious-smelling stuff.

"Mmm-mmm!" he says.
"Now, *this* is gumbo just like Maman used to make."

Maman's Spicy–Hot Gumbo
1. Heat one pot of water till it's boiling.
2. Throw in
   a mess of fresh crawdads,
   a load of tangy sliced okra,
   a sprinkle of tongue-searing spices,
   a heap of long-grained white rice.
3. Then add (if you have 'em on hand)
   Maman's special ingredients.
   (You know the ones. A little sass. Sass does
   make a gumbo tasty.)